Julia
the Sleeping Beauty Fairy

To Tabitha, Verity and Thalia, from the fairies

ORCHARD BOOKS
338 Euston Road, London NW1 3BH
Orchard Books Australia
Level 17/207 Kent Street, Sydney, NSW 2000
A Paperback Original

First published in 2015 by Orchard Books

HiT entertainment

A CIP catalogue record for this book is available
from the British Library.

ISBN 978 1 40833 648 9

1 3 5 7 9 10 8 6 4 2

Printed in Great Britain

FSC
www.fsc.org
MIX
Paper from
responsible sources
FSC® C104740

Orchard Books is an imprint of Hachette Children's Group
and published by The Watts Publishing Group Limited, an Hachette UK company.

www.hachette.co.uk

Julia
the Sleeping Beauty
Fairy

by Daisy Meadows

ORCHARD

www.rainbowmagic.co.uk

The Fairyland Palace

Fairytale Lane

Rachel's

Tippington Town

Jack Frost's
Ice Castle

Forest

Tiptop Castle

Jack Frost's Spell

The Fairytale Fairies are in for a shock!
Cinderella won't run at the strike of the clock.
No one can stop me – I've plotted and planned,
And I'll be the fairest Ice Lord in the land.

It will take someone handsome and witty and clever
To stop storybook endings for ever and ever.
But to see fairies suffer great trouble and strife,
Will make me live happily all of my life!

Contents

Over the Drawbridge

Rachel Walker rested her hand on the drawbridge chain of Tiptop Castle and looked down at the moat below. Her best friend, Kirsty Tate, was standing beside her, gazing at the elegant lawns and flower gardens that surrounded the castle. They had paused halfway across the drawbridge to admire the view.

"I feel like a princess standing here," said Kirsty in a dreamy voice. "It's just like something out of a fairy tale!"

"We're so lucky to be able to stay here for the Fairytale Festival," said Rachel, as the spring breeze ruffled her blonde hair.

It was half term, and Kirsty was staying with Rachel to share a very special treat. Tiptop Castle was a beautiful old castle on the edge of Tippington, and this year it was hosting the famous Fairytale Festival.

"I can't wait to see all the people dressed up as fairies and fairytale characters," said Kirsty.

"I wonder if we'll meet any *real* fairies," said Rachel.

The girls shared a happy smile. They

had been friends of the fairies ever since they met on Rainspell Island, and had shared many amazing adventures.

"Come on," said Kirsty. "Let's go inside."

The castle gatehouse was decorated with glimmering fairy lights. Inside was a festival organiser dressed as Puss-in-Boots. He waved his paw at Kirsty and Rachel, and then stroked his whiskers.

"Welcome to Tiptop Castle!" he said in a deep voice. "What are your names?"

The girls told him, and he ticked them off on his list. Then he gave them a big smile.

"Please enter the castle and explore with the other children until lunchtime," he said. "You can go anywhere you like and look at everything. Have fun!"

"This is going to be amazing!" said Rachel, hurrying inside and gazing around the grand entrance hall.

A chandelier hung from the ceiling,

thickly crusted with glittering crystals.
Twinkling fairy lights were twined
around the banisters of a gigantic
staircase, and suits of armour stood on
each side.

"Where shall we look first?" asked
Kirsty.

"Let's go upstairs," said Rachel, seizing
her best friend's hand. "I want to see
what a princess's bedroom looks like!"

Giggling, the girls ran up the staircase and discovered a long, wide corridor. All the doors were open, and they peeped inside each of them, gasping at what they saw. Every room was decorated in a different way. Rachel's favourite had golden furniture and red velvet curtains, while the one Kirsty liked best had a silver four-poster bed in the centre. It was surrounded by gauzy drapes and topped with a thick canopy of ivory satin. The curtains at the tall windows were azure blue.

"It looks like a mermaid's bedroom," she said with a happy sigh. "Look – the mirror is decorated with tiny silver seashells!"

All of the bedrooms took their breath away, and when they reached the end of the corridor they could hardly wait to see the rest of the castle. A second staircase led them back down to the ground floor, where they skidded across a polished oak floor into the drawing room.

"Look at the piano!" exclaimed
Rachel.

A beautiful white grand piano stood
beside the open French windows, and
the huge mirror over the fireplace made
the large room seem even bigger. Two

enormous sofas with clawed feet stood
beside the fireplace. There were tall
white lilies on every table.

"I wonder what's through there," said
Kirsty.

She pointed to a set of double doors
that led into another room. When they
walked through, the girls discovered a
long dining room, which had a huge
wooden banqueting table in the centre.
Candelabras were spaced out along the
length of the table, and portraits of kings
and queens filled the walls.

"This is just what I imagined a
fairytale castle would be like," said
Rachel. "They must have amazing feasts
in this room!"

Just then, they heard the sound of
laughter outside the room.

"That must be some of the other
children who are here for the festival,"
said Kirsty. "Let's go and say hello."

She went to the door of the dining
room and stepped back out into the

hallway, but no one was there. Rachel joined her, and they heard footsteps running up the staircase.

"They must have gone to explore the bedrooms," said Rachel. "Never mind – I'm sure we'll meet them later. Let's see where this door leads."

She turned the handle of the next door along, and they walked into a cosy reading room. Large, squashy armchairs were positioned around the room beside polished side tables filled with snacks and jugs of water. The walls were lined with shelves of books that reached all the way to the high ceiling, and the girls gazed up at them in delight.

"Look, there are ladders so you can reach the highest shelves," said Kirsty.

"Those reading chairs look really

comfy," said Rachel. "Let's choose some books and snuggle up in them."

She turned to the nearest shelf and gave a cry of surprise. One of the books was glowing! Feeling excited, Rachel pulled the book off the shelf and out fluttered Hannah the Happy Ever After Fairy!

Fairytale Lane

"Hello, Hannah!" exclaimed Rachel and Kirsty together.

"It's wonderful to see you both!" said Hannah, her eyes shining with pleasure. "I've come because I know how much you like reading, so I have a surprise for you."

She waved her wand, and there was a
tinkling sound as silver fairy dust sparkled
around them. The
girls shrank
to fairy size
and felt their
gossamer
wings
fluttering on
their backs. They
were filled with a delicious sense of
excitement as they realised that Hannah
was taking them to Fairyland.

In the blink of an eye, the reading
room had disappeared. Rachel and
Kirsty were standing on a narrow,
cobbled lane. There were four pretty
cottages spaced out along the lane, with
thatched roofs and roses and honeysuckle

twining around the doors. The smoke
that came from the chimneys sparkled
in all the colours of the rainbow, and a
mouth-watering smell of freshly baked
cakes hung in the air.

"Welcome to Fairytale Lane," said
Hannah.

As she spoke, the cottage doors opened
and four beautiful fairies peered out.

When they saw the girls, they came
hurrying over to say hello.

"These are the Fairytale Fairies,"
said Hannah with a beaming smile.
"Meet Julia the Sleeping Beauty Fairy,
Eleanor the Snow White Fairy, Faith
the Cinderella Fairy and Lacey the Little
Mermaid Fairy."

"It's lovely to meet you all," said

Rachel, smiling at the fairies. "I didn't
know that there were Fairytale Fairies!"

"Oh yes," said Julia, whose auburn
hair was tied in a loose bun. "Each of
us takes care of a fairy tale and the
characters in it."

"Without our care, the characters could
get lost and the stories would be empty,"
added Eleanor.

Faith squeezed Kirsty's hand and smiled
shyly.

"Hannah told us how much you like
fairy tales," she said. "We have a present
for you."

Lacey pulled a book from behind her
back and handed it to the girls. It was so
sparkly that it was hard to know whether
it was gold or silver, and the title was
written in swirly pink lettering:

The Fairies' Book of Fairy Tales

A silky pink
ribbon bookmark
dangled from the
spine.

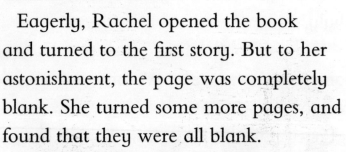

"Oh, thank you!"
said Kirsty in a
thrilled voice. "It's
the most beautiful
book I've ever seen!"

Eagerly, Rachel opened the book
and turned to the first story. But to her
astonishment, the page was completely
blank. She turned some more pages, and
found that they were all blank.

"I don't understand," said Julia, gazing
at the book in dismay.

She glanced over at her cottage
window, and then let out a cry of alarm.

"My magical jewellery box!" she exclaimed. "I always keep it on the sitting-room windowsill, but it's not there!"

Exchanging worried looks, the other three fairies dashed into their cottages. Seconds later they came back out, looking pale and anxious. All their magical objects had gone missing!

"This explains why *The Fairies' Book of Fairy Tales* is blank," said Julia with a groan. "But where could our magical objects be?"

"I can guess," said Kirsty suddenly. She pointed to the end of the lane, where four goblins were sneaking away! Each one of them had something clutched in his hands.

"They've stolen the magical objects!" Rachel guessed aloud. "Come on, we can catch them if we're quick!"

The girls zoomed off through the air
as fast as their wings could flutter, but
before they could reach the goblins, Jack
Frost leaped out in front of them!

"Halt!" he snarled. "Those fairy objects
are mine now, and I'm taking them to
the human world!"

"No," said Kirsty, trying to sound brave. "They belong to the Fairytale Fairies. You should give them back."

"Tough luck," Jack Frost snapped. "I've had enough of silly fairies and princesses. From now on, all fairy tales are going to be about me, me, ME!"

The goblins had stopped at the end of the lane, and they gave a big cheer when they heard what he said.

"Please stop!" cried Julia, flying up to join the girls. "Just think of all the children who won't have fairy tales to read."

"I don't care," said Jack Frost with a sneer. "And what's more, I'm going to start with *Sleeping Beauty*. From now on, it's going to be called *Sleeping Jack Frost!*"

As the girls gave horrified gasps, there was a thunderclap and, with a bolt of icy magic, Jack Frost and the goblins disappeared to the human world.

A Wooden Bed

Hannah and the Fairytale Fairies flew up to join Julia and the girls.

"Jack Frost has taken your magical objects to the human world," said Kirsty. "He's planning to make your fairy tales all about him, starting with *Sleeping Beauty*."

The fairies looked very upset.

"That means that the fairy tale characters must be in the human world too," said Julia. "We have to get our magical objects back and return the characters to their stories, or fairy tales will be ruined forever."

"Please let us help you," said Rachel. "We can't let Jack Frost do this to our favourite stories!"

The Fairytale Fairies looked very grateful, and Hannah nodded.

"I think it would be a good idea to help Julia first," she said.

"Oh yes, please," said Julia. "I need my magic jewellery box to rescue Sleeping Beauty and return her to her story."

"Then we should go back to the human world straight away and start searching," said Kirsty.

Julia nodded and, with a wave of her wand, she whisked all three of them back to Tiptop Castle. The girls found themselves standing in the cosy reading room, human-sized again. Julia fluttered between them.

"Where shall we start looking?" she asked in a breathless voice.

Before the girls could reply, they heard
laughter and giggles coming from the big
dining room next door.

"I wonder what's so funny," said
Kirsty.

"Let's go and find out," Rachel
suggested. "Julia, you can hide in my
pocket if you like."

Julia slipped into Rachel's pocket, and
then the girls ran through to the dining
room. They found a crowd of giggling
children wearing fairytale costumes –
from frog princes to enchanted princesses
and fairy godmothers. They were all
standing around the long banqueting
table, and Rachel and Kirsty had to
stand on tiptoes to see what they were
laughing at.

A beautiful young woman was lying in

the centre of the banqueting table, fast asleep. She was wearing a long golden gown with huge puffed sleeves, and her raven-black hair spread around her head in long, silky coils. Her skin looked as smooth as velvet.

"How on earth can she sleep through all this laughter?" Kirsty wondered aloud. "Who is she?"

"She's one of the festival organisers, of course," said a rather pompous girl dressed as a pumpkin. "Why else would she be wearing fancy dress?"

"It's a bit strange that she's fallen asleep on the table," said Rachel.

"Perhaps she's been working hard to prepare for the festival," Kirsty suggested.

"Come on, we have to start searching for the magical objects."

But as they moved towards the door, Julia peeped out of Rachel's pocket and then let out a squeak of surprise.

"That's not a festival organiser," whispered the little fairy. "That's Sleeping Beauty!"

Rachel and Kirsty stared at the princess, hardly able to believe that they were looking at the real Sleeping Beauty. Then Kirsty noticed something that made her heart thump. Four pairs of large, green feet were poking out from under the dining table!

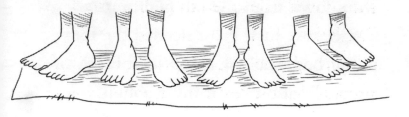

"Look!" Kirsty whispered, nudging Rachel. "Do those look like goblin feet to you?"

"Definitely," said Rachel with a frown. "Come on, let's get closer."

None of the other children had noticed the feet – they were all too busy giggling at Sleeping Beauty. Rachel and Kirsty crouched down beside the table and listened.

"My arms are aching from carrying that big girl," complained a scratchy voice.

"Mine too, said a deeper voice. "I don't see why we had to carry her all the way down from the big bedroom."

"Because Jack Frost needed the four-poster bed to be Sleeping Jack Frost, of course," squawked a third goblin voice.

"Talking of Jack Frost, shouldn't we get back upstairs?" said a fourth goblin, sounding nervous. "He might want something and he'll be ever so cross if we're not there."

"They're coming out," whispered Kirsty.

There was a scrabbling sound under the table, and then the girls saw the four goblins crawling out from under the table on their stomachs. They scuttled across the floor, unnoticed by the other children, and slipped out of the dining room.

"Quickly, let's follow them," said Rachel. "They can lead us to Jack Frost and the magical objects!"

Grumbling Goblins

Kirsty and Rachel hurried out of the dining room, and bumped straight into the man dressed as Puss-in-Boots, who had met them at the entrance.

"Aha, Rachel and Kirsty," he said. "Are you having fun exploring?"

The girls groaned inwardly as the goblins disappeared up the stairs.

"It's been really exciting so far," said Rachel. "We were just going to have another look upstairs."

"That's fine," said Puss-in-Boots. "But remember, we'll be serving lunch in the garden, so don't miss it!"

He walked on, and Rachel and Kirsty ran up the stairs. The landing was empty.

"They've gone into a bedroom," said Kirsty. "But which one?

Then they heard footsteps on the stairs behind them. They turned around and

saw a handsome young man dressed as
a prince coming towards them. He wore
a large felt hat with a
feather in it, and
his tunic was
made of gold
brocade.

"Good
morning," he
said, pulling
off his hat and
sweeping a low
bow. "I am Prince
Humphrey."

Rachel and Kirsty smiled at him,
guessing that he was another festival
organiser.

"We already know about the lunch
outside," said Rachel.

"Lunch outside?" repeated Prince Humphrey in a puzzled voice. "I don't know what you mean. I'm looking for Sleeping Beauty."

"That's the real prince from the fairy tale!" whispered Julia from Rachel's pocket.

"Oh my goodness, you've come to wake her up with a kiss, haven't you?" asked Kirsty in excitement. "She's downstairs in the dining room."

The prince darted back down the stairs, and the girls shared a smile before they hurried across the landing towards the bedrooms.

"Wait!" said Julia suddenly. "It will be easier to hide from Jack Frost if you are fairies too. Can you find a place to hide so that I can transform you?"

There was a large statue of a fairy on the landing, and Rachel pulled Kirsty behind it. Then Julia flew out and waved her wand. Instantly, the girls were fluttering their beautiful wings and hovering beside Julia. They checked that no one was coming and then zoomed towards the bedrooms.

"The goblins mentioned a four-poster bed," said Rachel. "So Jack Frost must be in the silver-and-blue room that you liked best, Kirsty."

The three fairies flew to the open door of the bedroom and peeped in. Jack Frost was lying on the beautiful silver bed, wearing a long blue nightgown and an old-fashioned nightcap. His head was buried in a plump pillow, and Rachel

noticed that his wand was lying on the ornate bedside table. The four goblins were lying on the floor around the bed, fidgeting and kicking each other. Each of them had a thin pillow, but they didn't look very sleepy.

"Get your foot out of my mouth, you clumsy oaf!" squawked one.

"Shan't!" said another, and then let out a yell of pain. "You bit me!"

Suddenly, Jack Frost
sat bolt upright as if
there were a spring
inside him.

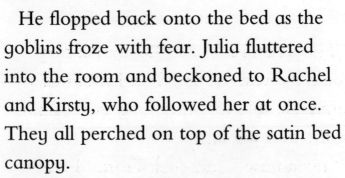

"You lot are too
noisy!" he roared
at the four goblins.
"How am I supposed
to sleep with all this
racket? SHUT UP!"

He flopped back onto the bed as the
goblins froze with fear. Julia fluttered
into the room and beckoned to Rachel
and Kirsty, who followed her at once.
They all perched on top of the satin bed
canopy.

"My pillow's too bumpy," muttered
one of the goblins.

"Mine's too squashy," said another.

"I'll have it," said a third, snatching at the pillow.

Rachel, Kirsty and Julia lay on their tummies and peered over the canopy.

"Any sign of my magical jewellery box?" whispered Julia.

The girls shook their heads. All they could see was the tassel on Jack Frost's nightcap, and the squirming green limbs of the four goblins.

"It's no use," said Jack Frost. "I can't sleep."

"We can't sleep either," wailed the goblins.

"Then you might as well give me your pillows," said Jack Frost. "Hand them over NOW!"

"It's not fair!" wailed the goblins as Jack Frost snatched their pillows. "You've already taken our blankets."

"I don't care about fair!" Jack Frost bellowed. "I care about ME! Now, sing me a lullaby."

"Oh no," groaned Rachel, who had heard the goblins singing before. "We might need earplugs."

Jack Frost sank back into the mound of pillows and the goblins linked arms and started to sing.

"Rock-a-bye Jack Frost on the soft bed.

When he shouts loud, it fills us with dread.

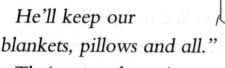

*When he
gets cross, the
snowflakes will fall.
He'll keep our
blankets, pillows and all."*

Their squawky voice made the fairies
wince. Jack Frost pulled his nightcap
down over his ears and plumped up his
pillow.

"Idiots!" he snarled. "Call that a
lullaby? Just shut up and lie down."

"Look!" hissed Kirsty.

As Jack Frost plumped up his pillow,
he revealed the corner of an engraved
wooden box hidden underneath it. Julia
sharply drew in her breath.

"That's my magical jewellery box!"
she exclaimed. "Thank goodness we've
found it! But how can we get it back?"

Pillow Fight!

The goblins lay down again, grumbling
under their breath. The fairies could only
catch a few muttered words.

"Stupid hard floors."

"No pillows."

"It's a bit nippy."

An idea suddenly popped into Rachel's
head, and she turned to Kirsty and Julia
with excitement in her eyes.

"Everyone loves a pillow fight," she whispered. "We just need a few more pillows…"

Julia laughed and flicked her wand. At once, a huge mound of soft pillows appeared beside the goblins, who gave loud cheers and flung themselves into the pile. The fairies zoomed down from the  canopy and Julia returned Kirsty and Rachel to their human form. Rachel picked up a pillow and gently threw it at the nearest goblin. He turned and glared

at her for a moment, then a huge, toothy
smile spread across his face.

"PILLOW FIGHT!" he yelled.

Seconds later, pillows were whizzing
through the air as fast as the goblins
could hurl them. They were throwing
them at each other as well as at the girls,
and Jack Frost started jumping up and
down on the bed in a rage.

"Stop it!" he shrieked. "I'm trying to
sleep!"

The girls couldn't help giggling as they flung pillows back at the goblins. Julia retreated to the canopy and magicked up more and more pillows, until the floor was completely hidden under them.

Feeling brave, Rachel took aim and hurled a pillow at Jack Frost's head. His nightcap came off and he shook his fist at her.

"We have to make him join in the fight and get him away from the magical jewellery box," Rachel panted.

Kirsty grabbed another pillow and flung it at Jack Frost with all her might. He fell over backwards and then bounced up again, scarlet with fury.

"You pesky humans!" he screeched.
"I'll make you sorry for disturbing me!"

He snatched up his plump pillow and
threw it at them as hard as he could,
revealing the magical jewellery box lying
on the mattress. The girls ducked the
pillow and Rachel dived towards the
bed. But Jack Frost was too quick for
her. With a sneering laugh he snatched
up the jewellery box, jumped down from
the bed and sprinted out of the room.

"After him!" Julia cried. "We mustn't let him get away again!"

Rachel and Kirsty pelted after Jack Frost, who had hitched his nightgown up over his knees so that he could run faster. Behind them, they could hear the patter of goblin feet. Julia zoomed above their heads.

"He's going downstairs!" she called. "Faster!"

The girls hurtled downstairs and chased Jack Frost into the dining room. He skidded around the enormous table and stood in the far corner, panting. The girls stopped to catch their breath too, and then noticed that Sleeping Beauty was no longer lying on the table. She was sitting up, and her lovely eyes were open. She was awake! Prince Humphrey was

standing beside the table and holding her
hand. They both looked at Jack Frost
and the girls in surprise.

"Where are the other children?" asked
Rachel, looking around.

"They went outside to have some
lunch," said Prince Humphrey.

Sleeping Beauty blinked a few times
and then spoke in a soft, musical voice.

"I'm a little confused," she said. "Where is my palace? Shouldn't I be in my bed?"

"It's all Jack Frost's fault," said Kirsty, looking at the Ice Lord. "He stole Julia's magical jewellery box. Without it, you can't get back into your own story! We've been trying to get it from him."

"In that case, please allow us to help you," said Sleeping Beauty.

She jumped down from the table at once, and Prince Humphrey turned to face Jack Frost.

"You'll never catch me," said Jack Frost, curling his lip. "A couple of little girls and two weedy fairytale characters are no match for the great Jack Frost!"

"We'll see about that," said Sleeping Beauty in a commanding voice. "I am a princess, and I insist that you give me that jewellery box right now!"

The Magical Jewellery Box

Prince Humphrey ran towards the Ice
Lord, who darted around the table
in the opposite direction. Sleeping
Beauty blocked his way, and he dodged
sideways, diving under the table and
scrambling out near the door. But
Rachel and Kirsty were there, and
he was forced to duck back under the

table again. Sleeping Beauty, Prince
Humphrey and the girls each crouched
down at one side of the table.

"There's no way out," said Rachel,
remembering what she had noticed in the
bedroom. "Your wand is upstairs where
you left it, so you can't escape by magic.
Give us the jewellery box and we will let
you go."

Just then, they heard the heavy patter
of bare feet behind them, and the four
goblins appeared in the doorway.

"Just in the nick of time," yelled Jack
Frost. "CATCH!"

He tossed the magical jewellery box
over Kirsty's head towards the door. But
Kirsty sprang into the air, reaching her
hands high above her head.

"Noooo!" shrieked Jack Frost as

Kirsty's right hand closed around the box.

"Yes!" Rachel cheered in delight. "You didn't know that Kirsty's the best netball player in her school!"

Smiling with relief, Kirsty handed the magical jewellery box to Julia, and it immediately shrank to fairy size. Jack Frost jumped up in fury and banged his head on the underside of the table. A large lump appeared under his spiky hair.

"You interfering, annoying humans!" he snapped, clutching his head and crawling out from under the table. "Just you wait until I've got my wand in my hand!"

"It's too late," said Rachel. "Julia has her magical object back."

Jack Frost stuck out his tongue at her and then stomped out of the room with the goblins.

"Thank you both for all your help," said Julia, holding her magical jewellery box close to her heart. "I'll never forget your kindness – or your courage!"

She blew them each a kiss and then disappeared back to Fairyland in a shimmering haze of fairy dust.

Prince Humphrey clasped Sleeping
Beauty in his arms as they started to
shimmer and fade.

"Goodbye!" Sleeping Beauty called.
"Thank you!"

Moments later they had gone and the
girls were alone in the
dining room.

"Do you think
they've returned
to their story?"
asked Kirsty.

"I hope so,"
said Rachel as
her stomach gave
a loud rumble. "But
right now, I think we
should go and get some lunch with the
others!"

That night, Rachel and Kirsty felt like princesses as they got ready for their first night at Tiptop Castle. Their bedroom was at the top of one of the tall castle towers, and the tiny arched windows looked out over the glassy lake and the beautiful moonlit gardens.

"This is the most incredible room I've ever slept in," said Kirsty.

She gazed around at the dark wooden furniture, which had been polished until it gleamed, and the single four-poster beds with their drapes and canopies. Rachel flopped down on her bed and yawned, snuggling back against her feathery pillow.

"It's been a wonderful day," she said. "Oh, what's this? There's something hard under my pillow... "

She reached her hand under her pillow and drew out the sparkling book that the fairies had given them – *The Fairies' Book of Fairy Tales*.

Kirsty gave a gasp of delight.

"I'd forgotten about our present in all the excitement," she said. "I wonder how it got there?"

"Magic," said Rachel with a grin.

Kirsty joined Rachel on her bed, and with their fingers crossed they opened the book and turned to the first story. They were relieved to see the words 'Sleeping Beauty' at the top of the page. The story was in the

book again, and Sleeping Beauty and
her prince were both back where they
belonged.

"Let's read it before bed," Rachel
suggested.

The girls loved the story and had read
it together often. But this time, when
they read about the party that the King
and Queen threw to celebrate Sleeping
Beauty being born, they discovered
something new. Kirsty leaned closer to
the picture.

"Look," she said in an awed tone. "Look at Sleeping Beauty's seven fairy godmothers."

Rachel leaned closer too, and then shared a thrilled smile with her best friend. The fairy godmothers were the Princess Fairies!

When they reached 'happily ever after', Rachel couldn't resist turning the page to see if the next story had reappeared too.

"It's blank," she said with a sigh. "The other stories are still missing, and we have three more Fairytale Fairies to help."

Kirsty put her arm around Rachel's shoulders and smiled at her.

"Don't worry," she said. "As long as best friends like us stick together, I know that we can make a happy ending!"

Meet the
Fairytale Fairies

Julia
the Sleeping Beauty
Fairy

Eleanor
the Snow White
Fairy

Faith
the Cinderella
Fairy

Lacey
the Little Mermaid
Fairy

Kirsty and Rachel are going to a Fairytale Festival!
Can they help get the Fairytale Fairies' magical objects
back from Jack Frost, before he ruins all the stories?

www.rainbowmagicbooks.co.uk

**Now it's time for Kirsty and
Rachel to help...**

Eleanor the Snow White Fairy

Read on for a sneak peek...

When Kirsty Tate opened her eyes, for
a moment she couldn't remember where
she was. She gazed up at the canopy
that hung over her four-poster bed. A
spring breeze had wafted open the gauzy
curtains, and the sun lit up the white
dressing table with its gold and silver
swirls. On the dressing table lay a book
with a sparkling cover – *The Fairies'
Book of Fairy Tales.*

A smile spread across Kirsty's face as
she remembered everything that had
happened the day before. She sat up and
looked across to where her best friend,

Rachel Walker, was still fast asleep.

"Rachel, wake up," she said in a gentle voice. "It's our second day at Tiptop Castle!"

Rachel opened her eyes and gave Kirsty a sleepy smile. They were staying in a beautiful old castle on the outskirts of Tippington, where the Fairytale Festival was being held. Their bedroom was at the top of a tower of the castle, and the girls had agreed that it was fit for a princess – or two!

"What are you going to wear today?" asked Kirsty, hopping out of bed and opening the enormous wardrobe where they had hung their clothes.

"How about our fairy dresses?" suggested Rachel, swinging her legs out of bed. "It'd be fun to join in with everyone else."

The day before, all the festival organisers had been wearing fairytale fancy dress. Kirsty clapped her hands together.

"That's a great idea," she said, "especially after our Fairyland visit yesterday!"

As they pulled on their beautiful fairy dresses, they talked about the adventure they had shared with Julia the Sleeping Beauty Fairy.

Read **Eleanor the Snow White Fairy** to find out what adventures are in store for Kirsty and Rachel!

Competition!

The Fairytale Fairies have created a special
competition just for you!

Collect all four books in the Fairytale Fairies series
and answer the special questions in the back of each one.

Once you have all the answers, take the first letter from
each one and arrange them to spell a secret word!
When you have the answer, go online and enter!

**Jack Frost lives in the
Ice** _ _ _ _ _ _

We will put all the correct entries into a draw and select
a winner to receive a special Rainbow Magic Goody Bag
featuring lots of treats for you and your fairy friends.
You'll also feature in a new Rainbow Magic story!

Enter online now at www.rainbowmagicbooks.co.uk

Join in the magic online by signing up
to the Rainbow Magic fan club!

Meet the fairies, play games and
get sneak peeks at the latest books!

There's fairy fun for everyone at

www.rainbowmagicbooks.co.uk

You'll find great activities, competitions, stories and
fairy profiles, and also a special newsletter.

Find a fairy with
your name!